Baby Bat's Lullaby

For Syd, my baby bat

—J.M.

For Clyde Bulla

—J.N.

Baby Bat's Lullaby
Text copyright © 2004 by Jacquelyn Mitchard
Illustrations copyright © 2004 by Julia Noonan
Manufactured in China by South China Printing Company Ltd.
All rights reserved.
www.harperchildrens.com

Library of Congress Cataloging-in-Publication Data
Mitchard, Jacquelyn.
 Baby bat's lullaby / by Jacquelyn Mitchard ; illustrated by Julia Noonan. — 1st ed.
  p.   cm.
 Summary: With loving words, a mother bat lulls her baby to sleep.
 ISBN 0-06-050760-8 — ISBN 0-06-050761-6 (lib. bdg.)
 [1. Bats—Fiction. 2. Lullabies—Fiction. 3. Bedtime—Fiction.] I. Noonan, Julia, ill.
II. Title.
PZ7.M6848Bab 2004   2002010978
[E]—dc21   CIP
                                                                             AC

Typography by Elynn Cohen   1 2 3 4 5 6 7 8 9 10   ❖   First Edition

The art was made with acrylic and oil paints on paper.

JACQUELYN MITCHARD

Baby Bat's Lullaby

illustrated by JULIA NOONAN

HarperCollins*Publishers*

Go to sleep,
Small new prince of the dark,
Quick dancer in the sky park,

Field squeaker,
Forest streaker,

Little wings petal-light,
Little teeth sugar-white.

My darling night creeper,
All-morning sleeper,
My baby bat.

Go to sleep,
Barn-hall glider,
Twilight slider,

Mosquito frightening,
Swift as lightning,

Dearer than night,
Brown eyes bright,

My jewel so soft,
My dancer aloft,
My baby bat.

Sleep beside me,
Master flyer,

Upside-down clinger,
Little-toe swinger,

Wings wrapped tight,
Cuddle till night.

Under Mama's soft gaze
Dream away dozy days,
For at dusk we shall play.

Strong little sweetling,
Mama's best treatling,

Sleep, little
Fleet little
Dear baby bat.